Mr Brush
(The brush seller)

Anna, Mrs Luigi and **Mr Luigi, Alex** and **Roberta**
(Mrs Luigi makes the pizzas, Mr Luigi makes the ice cream)

Noah
(The tropical fisherman)

Mrs Pankhurst
(And Henrietta)

This is Migloo.

Benny
(He doesn't do much...)

And this is the story of Migloo's day.

Molly
(She makes the orange juice)

Roshan
(The traffic policeman)

Juan and **Conchita**
(He goes down holes, she goes up poles)

Lotti and **Noggin** and **Kitty** and **Toto**
(Noggin thinks he's a Viking and Kitty thinks she's a cat)

Flossy
(The candyfloss lady)

Boris
(He sticks up posters)

Basil
(He sells the doughnuts)

Mia
(She puts up the aerials)

Charlie
(The newspaper man)

Dr Whom
(She is Sunnytown's doctor)

Dougal
(He drives the fork-lift truck)

Farmer Tom and **Suki**
(From Sunnytown Farm)

Terry and **Bea** and **Lizzy**
(Terry and Bea run Sunnytown's taxi service)

Miss Othmar
(She teaches at the school)

Polly
(She works at the factory)

William Bee

Gwendolyn and **Cecily**
(Or is it the other way round?)

Eric and **Ernie**
(Brother builders)

Sebastian
(He works at the factory)

Mr Tompion
(The clock winder)

Zebedee
(The Fancy Dress man)

"The Great Fernando"
(And Milo the Monkey)

Zoë
(She works at the factory)

Harry and **Alphonso**
(The Sunnytown firemen)

Freda and **Bobby** and **Olivia** and **Bert**
(From Sunnytown garage)

François and **Agatha**
(They deliver the post)

Mr McGregor and **Rose**
(They grow lots of plants)

Mr and **Mrs Smudge** and **Scruff**
(The messiest family in town)

Isabella
(The traffic police lady)

Reg
(Sells the veg)

Otto
(He's always around)

Indira
and **Flopsy** and **Tiny Mouse**

Mr and **Mrs Dickens**
(He sells books and she teaches with them)

Lenny
(He sweeps up)

Sydney and **Lily** and **Florence**
(He cleans the windows and Florence bakes the bread)

Dylan
(The school caretaker)

Daisy and **Felix** and **Amit**
(Sandwiches, carpets and rugs)

Migloo's Day

by william bee

Sunnytown
Twinned with Sillycone Valley

With special thanks to:
Art Director, **Audrey Keri-Nagy**,
and Editor, **Maria Tunney**.
Also to: **Jane Winterbotham**,
Deirdre McDermott, **Alice Blacker**,
Sue Tarsky and **Jodie Hodges**.

Migloo's up nice and early this morning
and he's feeling rather hungry...

"You look like you're ready for breakfast,
Migloo!" says Farmer Tom. "I'm off to the
market, why don't you hop on?"
Migloo wags his tail, which means,
'Yes please!'

AT THE MARKET

Migloo thanks Farmer Tom with a wag of his tail and then he sets off to explore the market. It's full of people selling all sorts of things – brushes, flowers, silly china cats and ... mmmm, there are lots and lots of delicious smells!

AT THE TOWN SQUARE

Migloo can smell Molly's ripe, zingy oranges and Florence's just-baked crusty bread. And he can also smell his FAVOURITE smell of all ... Suki's Super! Sizzling! Sausages! But can Migloo find them?

? QUESTION TIME ?

Where's Tiny Mouse?
Who's on a ladder?
Who has lost a shoe?
Has Henrietta laid an egg?

Oh yes! Migloo certainly has a good nose – especially
for sausages!
"Hello Migloo! I've made these just for you," says Suki.
Migloo wags his tail, ever such a lot,
which means, 'Thank you, Suki,
I do love sausages –
ever such a lot!'

After all that breakfast Migloo
would like something sweet...

"One of my famous Knickerbocker Glories!" says Mr Luigi.
Migloo is delighted! He wags his tail which, of course,
means, 'Thank you, Mr Luigi, this is the best
Knickerbocker Glory EVER!'

Who has Migloo spotted now? It's Zebedee! He has all sorts of fancy dresses and fancy suits, and fancy hats and fancy boots. Migloo likes trying on hats. This one has a big feather on it – PIRATE MIGLOO!

What a great start to Migloo's day! And now Sydney offers Migloo a ride in his side car.

"Jump in, Migloo," says Sydney. "I'm off to the plastics factory. It's got a LOT of dirty windows."

Migloo wags his tail, which means, 'Smashing!'

AT THE PLASTICS FACTORY

Migloo and Sydney arrive at the plastics factory — it's a very busy place! It's noisy, too! There are big, noisy machines and big, noisy lorries and a big, noisy fork-lift truck. So will Migloo be able to hear the bell that means ... IT'S LUNCHTIME!?

MUSIC CONCERT NIGHT!

Building Supplies

JR 70

☎ 222 21 46 49

5

international plastics

POST OFFICE

FIRE STATION

FARM

SCHOOL

Building Supplies

9 ✳

FOR HIRE

SUNNYTOWN NEWS

JS 64

TAXI

62 68

factory shop

? QUESTION TIME ?

Can you see a bell?

Who has swapped hats?

Can you find Cecily?

And who's reading?

SUNNYTOWN NEWS

RUBBER DUCKS MAKE BID FOR FREEDOM!

READ ALL ABOUT IT!

PIZZA

Oh yes! Migloo's ears are almost as good as his nose. Daisy makes sandwiches for everyone at the plastics factory. "And I've got one extra for my little friend Migloo," she says.

Daisy and Migloo take some sandwiches over to Dougal, the fork-lift truck driver.

"Tomato and lettuce? Mmmm, my favourite," says Dougal. Migloo wags his tail, which means, 'Mine too!'

Next door is the builders' yard.
Eric is stacking tiles in his wheelbarrow.
"Hi Migloo, can you sit on top so they don't slip off?"
Migloo wags his tail, which means, 'Certainly, as
long as I can wear a hard hat
in case *I* slip off.'

François has just collected a mysterious parcel from
Polly at the plastics factory and spots
Migloo in his hard hat.
"That hat looks perfect for
a motorbike ride! Jump on
Migloo and hold on tight!"

AT THE FIRE STATION

Migloo jumps down from the motorbike and quickly picks up the scent of something JAMMY and DOUGHY and NUTTY. What could it be? Migloo heads in the direction of the fire station. There he finds his friends, Harry and Alphonso, and – aha! – delicious jam doughnuts!

14:30

TRAFFIC POLICE

FIRE SERVICE

AMBULANCE SERVICE

EMERGENCY SERVICES

GO SLO

GO!

GO HO GIVE UP

TRAFFIC POLICE

POST OFFICE

AIRPORT

SCHOOL

FARM

9

AMBULANCE SERVICE

A 022 DX

A 022 DX

DIAL 329

TAXI

A1 TAXIS

SUNNYTOWN NEWS

CHEEKY MONKEY ON THE LOOSE WITH STOLEN HAT!

READ ALL ABOUT IT!

"How about a nice cup of tea, Migloo?" asks Alphonso. Migloo wags his tail, which means, 'Yes please – if it comes with a nice jam doughnut!'

After tea and doughnuts, Migloo helps Roshan and Isabella load road signs into the police jeep. The signs are very bossy: STOP! GO LEFT! GO RIGHT! GIVE WAY! GIVE UP!

Behind the police station Roshan shows Migloo what happens
when drivers fail to: STOP! GO LEFT! GO RIGHT! GIVE WAY!
GIVE UP!

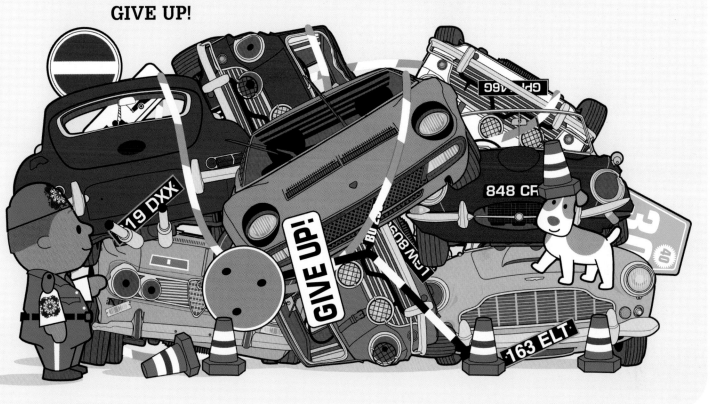

Roshan asks Migloo if he would like to come for a ride.
Migloo wags his tail, which means, 'Yes PLEASE
Mr policeman, SIR!'

AT SUNNYTOWN SCHOOL

How exciting! Roshan and Isabella are visiting the school for 'Don't Fall Off Your Bike Week'. Migloo is very keen to help. But first he MUST visit Mrs Luigi's cafe. She always has a special snack just for Migloo and today it's a slice of her homemade pepperoni pizza!

? QUESTION TIME ?

Who's holding a balloon?
Who has some doughnuts?
Where's Little White Owl?

BEWARE CHILDREN!

LIBRARY

ALL THE LATEST BOOKS

POST

MH•588

GO SLOW!

GO AWAY!

Elephant Fuels

A069 DX

TRAFFIC POLICE

222 31 87 71

After his pizza, Migloo helps Roshan and Isabella with the children's bike safety lesson. It's dangerous work ... the new cones that François brought from the plastics factory are all getting SQUASHED!

Here is Lily ... squashing a cone.

Here is Alex ... squashing a cone.

And here are Lottie and Anna ... squashing each other.

Migloo decides it's safer indoors where the
children in the art class are making fancy hats.
Felix has made a hat for him and Migloo is very
pleased with it – KING MIGLOO!

The bell sounds for home time, but today
the children are going somewhere special.
Miss Othmar and Mrs Dickens invite
Migloo to come, too.
Migloo wags his tail, which means,
'That would be nice – as long as I
can wear my hat.'

AT THE GARAGE

They've stopped at the garage...
There's something wrong with the school bus!
The engine is smoking and oil is running out from underneath.
"OH, NO!" cry the children. Migloo rushes off to find Bert, the chief mechanic.

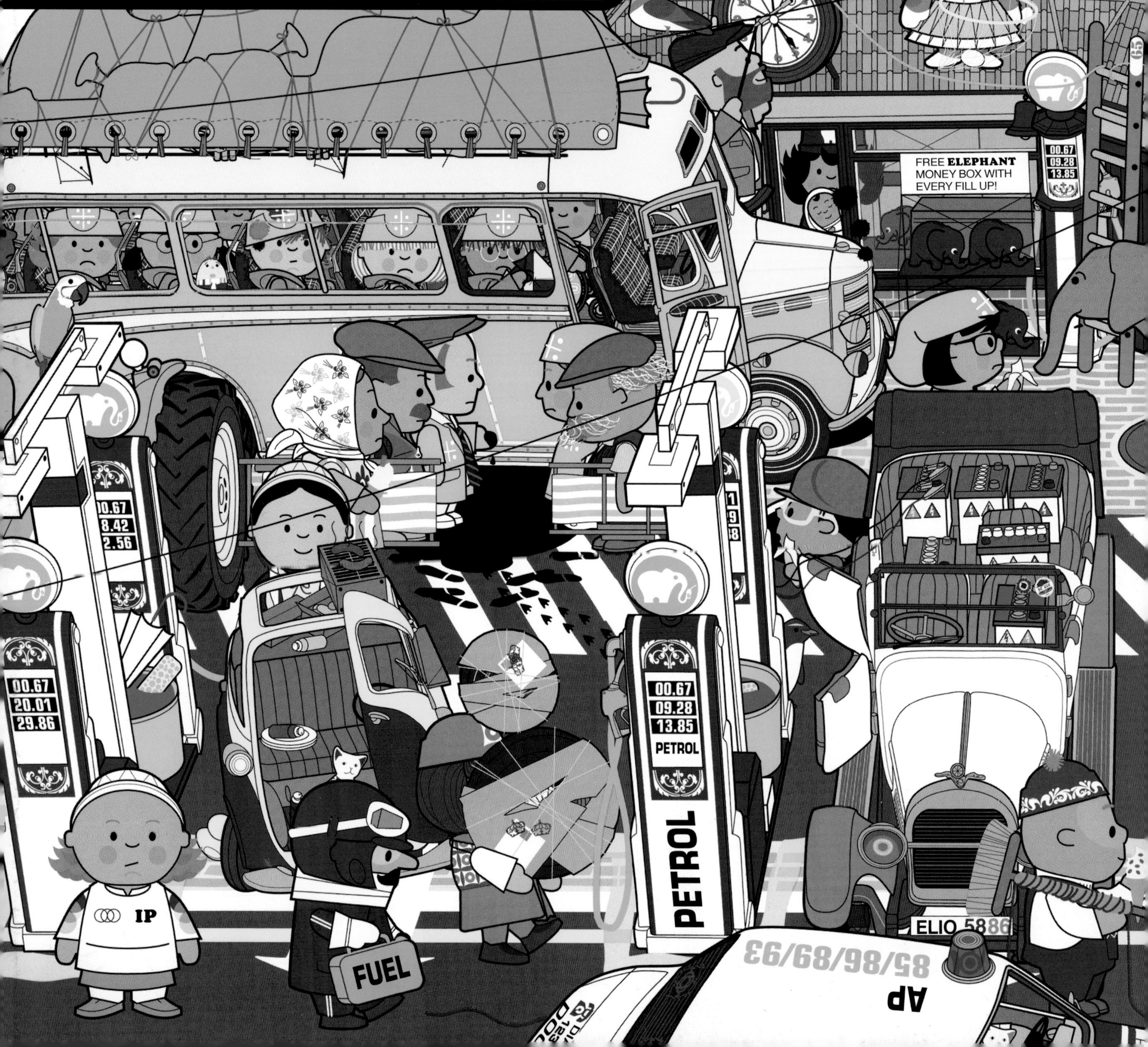
Eleph
FREE ELEPHANT MONEY BOX WITH EVERY FILL UP!
00.67
09.28
13.85
00.67
20.01
29.86
00.67
09.28
13.85
PETROL
PETROL
IP
FUEL
ELIO 5886
85/86/89/93
AP

"All right, Migloo?" says Bert.

Migloo runs around Bert barking and wagging his tail, which means, 'The school bus has broken down and all the children are very upset!'

"Look at all that SMOKE, Bert! Can you fix it?" asks Miss Othmar.

GOODNESS! LOOK! Everyone's come to the rescue!
But where could they all be going?

Bert puts the bus up on the ramp and pokes about with his spanner.

"Oh dear. It looks like your big end has gone! It will take AGES to fix."

No one knows what to do!
But Migloo – who has had a lovely day being driven about by all his friends, and fed sausages and ice creams, sandwiches and pizza – suddenly has an idea!

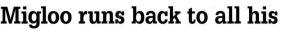

Migloo runs back to all his friends, wagging his tail, which, of course, mea

THIS WAY
PLEASE!
←

NL 75778

GO RIGHT!
THEN LEFT!

GO!

QUICK!

'The school bus has broken down! The children need your help!'

AT SUNNYTOWN PARK

The music concert, of course! With a front
row seat for Migloo! He settles down to listen
to the music and wags his tail, which either
means, 'It's great that all my friends were
able to help the children get to their concert
and play their instruments!' OR 'What I really
fancy right now ... is a nice plate of CHIPS!'

PIZZA
PIZZA

intern
plastic

SUNNYTOWN NEWS

William Bee's Busy Page

Sunnytown is such a busy place. There's always so much going on! There are lots and lots of people working, eating, driving and playing which means ... there are lots and lots of things for YOU to look out for!

What's wrong with Migloo?

1 2 3 4 5

ANSWERS: 1. No eyebrows! 2. Five legs! 3. Extra eyebrows! 4. 'Where's my tail?' 5. Missing patch!

Who's in the tree?

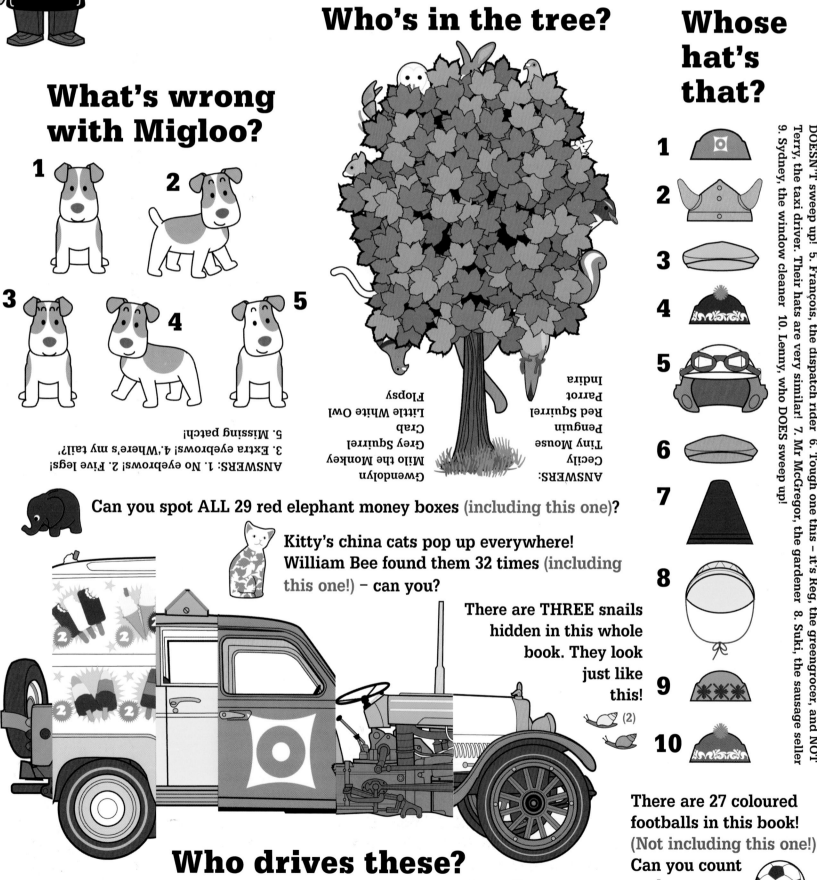

ANSWERS:
Gwendolyn
Milo the Monkey
Grey Squirrel
Little White Owl
Flopsy
Crab
Cecily
Tiny Mouse
Penguin
Red Squirrel
Parrot
Indira

Whose hat's that?

1 2 3 4 5 6 7 8 9 10

ANSWERS: 1. Agatha, the post lady 2. Noggin, the Viking 3. Dylan, the school caretaker 4. Benny, who DOESN'T sweep up! 5. François, the dispatch rider 6. Tough one this – it's Reg, the greengrocer, and NOT Terry, the taxi driver. Their hats are very similar! 7. Mr McGregor, the gardener 8. Suki, the sausage seller 9. Sydney, the window cleaner 10. Lenny, who DOES sweep up!

Can you spot ALL 29 red elephant money boxes (including this one)?

Kitty's china cats pop up everywhere! William Bee found them 32 times (including this one!) – can you?

There are THREE snails hidden in this whole book. They look just like this!

(2)

There are 27 coloured footballs in this book! (Not including this one!) Can you count each one you see?

Who drives these?

ANSWERS: 1. Roshan, the traffic policeman 2. Mr Luigi, the ice cream man 3. Terry, the taxi driver 4. Agatha, the post lady 5. Farmer Tom 6. William Bee

What are we looking at here?

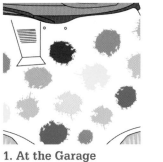
1. At the Garage

2. At Sunnytown Park

3. At Sunnytown School

4. At the Town Square

5. At the Market

Who carries one of these?

1

2

3

5

4

6

7

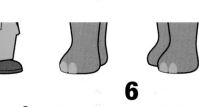
8

Who do these legs belong to?

1　　2　　3　　4　　5　　6

What are these?

Whose  bike is this?

On the pages where you see William Bee, holding his yellow 'QUESTION TIME' sign, it means there are LOTS of things to find!

And if you feel like getting even BUSIER, you can find the answers to ALL the questions he asks below on EACH and EVERY one of the 8 pages where his yellow 'QUESTION TIME' sign appears!

So, that means: you can find Flopsy 8 times and missing shoes in 8 different places! And lots of people eating bananas and wearing glasses. Phew … that IS busy!

Busy Bee Questions

Here are all the things to find and how many times to find them in total!

Who's reading? (13) Who's on a ladder? (24) Who has lost a shoe? (9) Has Henrietta laid an egg? (8 times!) Who's holding an ice cream or a lolly? (21) And who's DROPPED an ice cream? (2) Who's wearing glasses? (68) Who's holding a balloon? (8) Who has some doughnuts? (26) CAN YOU SEE: Migloo? (8) Butterfly? (8) Tiny Mouse? (8) A bell? (9) The pink knitting? (10) Cecily and Gwendolyn? (8 each) Indira? (8) Red Squirrel and Grey Squirrel? (8 each) Little White Owl? (8) Penguin? (8) Mr Smudge – usually just his sooty brush? (8) Milo the Monkey? (8) Flopsy? (8) An umbrella? (9) Parrot? (8) Who has swapped hats? Who's eating a banana? AND... What's Crab holding?

Goodbye Migloo.

See you again soon.

First published 2015 by Walker Books Ltd, 87 Vauxhall Walk, London SE11 5HJ • This edition published 2016 • © 2015 William Bee • 10 9 8 7 6 5 4 3 2 1 • The right of William Bee to be identified as author/illustrator of this work has been asserted by him in accordance with the Copyright, Designs and Patents Act 1988 • This book has been typeset in URW Egyptienne, Cooper Five Opti Black, VAG Rounded, Eurostile, Helvetica, Textile • Printed in China • All rights reserved. No part of this book may be reproduced, transmitted or stored in an information retrieval system in any form or by any means, graphic, electronic or mechanical, including photocopying, taping and recording, without prior written permission from the publisher. • British Library Cataloguing in Publication Data: a catalogue record for this book is available from the British Library • ISBN 978-1-4063-6560-3 • www.walker.co.uk

www.miglooworld.com **migloo**